characters created by
lauren child

Say
Cheese

PUFFIN

Charlie and Lola™

Text based on the script
written by Samantha Hill

Illustrations from the TV animation

produced by Tiger Aspect

PUFFIN BOOKS
Published by the Penguin Group: London, New York, Australia,
Canada, India, Ireland, New Zealand and South Africa
Penguin Books Ltd, Registered Offices: 80 Strand, London WC2R 0RL, England

puffinbooks.com

First published 2007
This edition published 2008
3 5 7 9 10 8 6 4 2

Made and printed in China
ISBN: 978-1-856-13189-6

This edition produced for The Book People Ltd,
Hall Wood Avenue, Haydock, St Helens WA11 9UL

I have this little sister Lola.
She is small and very funny.
Today the school photographer is coming
and it is Lola's first ever school photo.

Lola says,
    "Mum said it is going to be
an EXTREMELY special photograph.
        Especially if I stay all tidy and clean."
                I say,
            "And how easy do you
                think THAT will be, Lola?"

            "It'll be easy peasy,
        lemon squeezy," says Lola.

"I can be really tidy and clean
for my school photograph. I can, Charlie.
Look at all these photographs on holiday
at Granny and Grandpa's."

"I didn't get chocolate spread on my dress!" says Lola.

I say,
"No, not on your dress, Lola…

What about this one in the park?"

Lola says,
"But I didn't get my shoes dirty!"

"No, that's because you took them off, Lola!"

"And look at your hair in this one."

Lola says,
"My face is all clean...
and look at my big
smile. Mum always says
I'm a good smiler!"

I say,
"Yep, you're a great
smiler... and what do you say
for a big smile?"

Lola says,

"Say Cheese! Cheese!
Cheese!"

When it's time to go to school,
    Lola says,
"Mum and me found my nicest skirt
and these are my best shoes
        and my favourite hairclips.

So you see, Charlie,
it will be a lovely
    school photograph."

In the playground, Lola sees Lotta.
Lola says,
"On the way to school I didn't even splash
in one single puddle."

"Neither did I!" says Lotta.

"I think I will look the most tidiest person
in the school photograph."
says Lola.

"Yes, you will,"
says Lotta,
"maybe…"

"Come on, Lotta," says Lola.
"Let's just play one
game of puddles."
Lotta says,
"I told my mum I would not
jump in any puddles."

"OK then," says Lola. "Let's play run around the puddles."

"See, when you run round you can stay all nice and clean!"

Then the bell goes for the start of school.

In the classroom, Lola says,
"I like my book. Do you like your book, Lotta?"
"Yes, but I do like the water tray too."

Lola says, "But reading is more tidy."
Lotta says, "Maybe we could play with something else?"

Then Lola says,
"What about the water tray?"

"Yes, yes, yes!"

At lunchtime, Lola says,
"Now I'm going
        to drink my pink milk,

very,
    very
        carefully."

Back in the classroom, Lola says,
    "I love painting."

"Me too," says Lotta. "It is my best thing.
    I'm sure we can stay all clean
        with our aprons on."

"I'm sure too," says Lola.
      "Just one finger each."

      "Careful, Lola..."

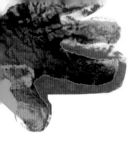
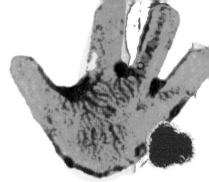

Then Lola says,
"Urgh… Lotta, my hands
are all blue."

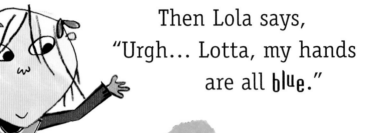

And Lotta says,
    "My hands are a bit
green and a bit red."

"But paint washes off,
    doesn't it?" says Lola.

    "Oh yes!" says Lotta.
        "Paint washes off!"

When Lotta goes to
    wash her hands,
Lola says,
    "I just want to
have one look
    at my lovely
painting!"

Then it's time
    for the school photo.

"Wait, Lotta!
I MUST have clean hands!"
    says Lola.

    "Wait for me!"

When we're waiting for our turn
to have our photo taken,

Lola says,
"Look how **clean** my hands
are, Charlie."

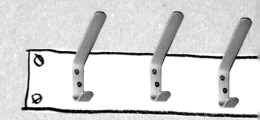

I say, "Just remember to **smile**."

"Oh yes," says Lola,
"I nearly forgot… I'm a good **smiler!**"

Then it's our turn.

I say, "Stay still, Lola.
Stop wriggling. Ready?"

"Whoops!" says Lola.

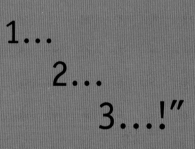

Then I say,
"And again. Ready,

1...
   2...
      3...!"

"Oh!" says Lola.

"Cheeese!"

Later, we look at
our school photographs.
I say, "Well, at least you're smiling, Lola!"

"But I'm NOT clean and I'm NOT tidy,
and I did try."

Lola says, "I just wanted one photograph
so Mum would be pleased."

"But Mum will be pleased," I say.

Lola says, "But I wanted Mum to be pleased
because I was all tidy and clean."

And then I had
an idea...

Dad said we could use
some of the old photos ...

After lots of
cutting
and snipping
and sticking,

Lola and I say...

"There!"

At bedtime, Lola comes into our room
with the special photo.

I say, "What did Mum say?"

"Mum says I REALLY am
a VERY good smiler,"
says Lola.

"Cheese!"